# Colors of the Wind

From Disney's
POCAHONTAS

# *Colors of the Wind*

Music by Alan Menken
Lyrics by Stephen Schwartz

HYPERION

New York

*You think I'm an ignorant savage,*

*And you've been so many places,*

*I guess it must be so.*

*But still I cannot see,*
*if the savage one is me,*

*How can there be*
*so much that you*
*don't know?*

*You don't know . . .*

*You think you own
whatever land you land on;*

*The earth is just a dead thing
you can claim;*

*But I know ev'ry rock and
tree and creature*

*Has a life, has a spirit,
has a name.*

*You think
the only people
who are people*

*Are the people
who look and
think like you,*

*But if you walk*
*the footsteps of a stranger*

*You'll learn things*
*you never knew you never knew.*

*Have you ever
heard the wolf cry
to the blue corn moon,*

*Or asked the
grinning bobcat
why he grinned?*

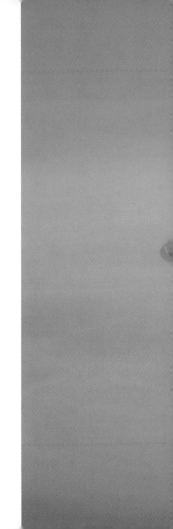

*Can you sing with all
the voices
of the mountain?*

*Can you paint with all the colors of the wind?*

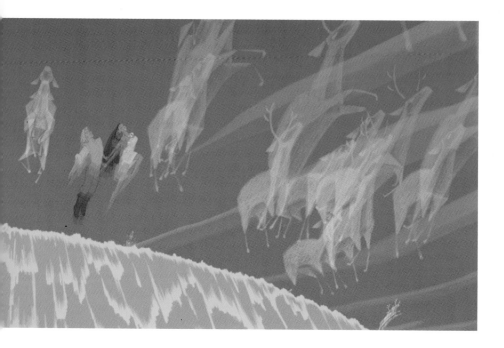

*Can you paint with all the colors of the wind?*

*Come run the hidden
pine trails of the forest,*

*Come taste the sun-sweet
berries of the earth;*

*Come roll in all the riches
all around you,*

*And for once, never wonder
what they're worth.*

*The rainstorm
and the river
are my brothers;*

*The heron
and the otter
are my friends;*

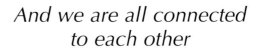

*And we are all connected
to each other*

*In a circle, in a hoop
that never ends.*

*How high does the*
*sycamore grow?*

*If you cut it down*
*then you'll never know.*

*And you'll never
hear the wolf cry
to the blue corn moon,*

*For whether
we are white
or copper-skinned,*

*We need to sing
with all the voices
of the mountain,*

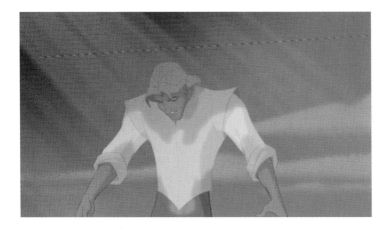

*Need to paint with all the colors of the wind.*

*You can own the earth
and still*

*all you'll own is earth
until*

*You can paint
with all the
colors of the wind.*

FOR INFORMATION ADDRESS:
HYPERION, 114 FIFTH AVENUE, NEW YORK, NY 10011

PRODUCED BY:
WELCOME ENTERPRISES, INC., 575 BROADWAY, NEW YORK, NY 10012

DESIGN BY JON GLICK

Library of Congress Cataloging-in-Publication Data
Schwartz, Stephen.
Colors of the wind / lyrics by Stephen Schwartz.
p.  cm.
"Music by Alan Menken."
At head of title: From Disney's Pocahontas.
ISBN 0-7868-6151-7
1. Indians of North America--Poetry.  2. Nature--Poetry.
I. Menken, Alan.  II. Pocahontas (Motion picture)  III. Title.
PS3569.C5675C65  1995
811' .54--dc20                              95-3191
                                             CIP

2  4  6  8  10  9  7  5  3  1

PRINTED IN SINGAPORE
BY TIEN WAH PRESS